George A. Spink

The Ackley Pilgrims

George A. Spink

The Ackley Pilgrims

ISBN/EAN: 9783337289614

Printed in Europe, USA, Canada, Australia, Japan

Cover: Foto ©Andreas Hilbeck / pixelio.de

More available books at **www.hansebooks.com**

THE ACKLEY PILGRIMS.

Nine Weeks Trip Through Europe,

Summer of '92.

BY

MRS. GEORGE A. SPINK,

A PILGRIM.

AUBURN, R. I.

PROVIDENCE, R. I.
PRESS OF THE J. C. HALL COMPANY.
1894.

This little book is respectfully dedicated to

Rev. Wm. N. Ackley,

in appreciation of his loving kindness as leader of

the

"Ackley Pilgrims."

By the Author.

PREFACE.

This work has not been written friends
  For profit, or for fame,
Or to secure publicity,
  Or make myself a name.

I simply wrote because I loved
  The countries, where we'd been,
And 'twas a pleasure to recall
  The beauties we had seen.

At the request of many friends
  I to the public give
This simple little truthful work,
  And trust 'twill pleasure give,—

To all, who read the simple tale
  Of the little "Ackley Band"
Who wandered far from home,
  "Innocents" in foreign land.

5

I trust the public will be kind
  To one who offers here
Her travels in poetic form
  With hesitation, fear,—

And over-look the many faults
  In this her first attempt.
To please has been her only wish,
  From all else she's exempt.

Signed,

Very Respectfully,

MRS. GEORGE A. SPINK.

THE VOYAGE.

'TWAS the steamship "City of Chester,"
   That sailed the summer sea,
And carried a goodly number
   Of innocents who would flee
From dull care or sordid pleasure,
   Leave friends and home behind,
Visit many foreign countries,
   Study and improve the mind.

Our kind leader, Reverend Ackley,
   With his wife so sweet and mild,
And professors without number,
   With one solitary child,
Married ladies, youths and misses,
   Doctors, ministers and such,
Assembled on that ship's deck
   To test old Neptune's touch.

Very soon his powers were tested,
   As the tides did ebb and flow,
And many a youth and maiden
   Were obliged to go below,

7

Where the stewardess, good woman,
  Often lent a helping hand
To assist them to their state-rooms,
  As they felt too weak to stand.

After days of relaxation,
  Lying low and keeping quiet,
They ascended to the deck again,
  Where they took a little diet,
Of beef-tea, a ginger-snap or two,
  An orange or an ice,
With sea-bread, hard as any stone,
  Or perhaps a little rice.

In nine cases out of every ten
  They recovered very fast,
And walked or ran around the deck
  Up to the very last,
When the coast of Ireland came in view,
  After ten days out at sea,
Ah! we felt like old Columbus,
  Though we laughed so merrily.

IRELAND.

FAIR Queenstown was the harbor
  Where we landed near the dawn,
In a drizzling rain we anchored
  On that well remembered morn;
Entered Custom House quite gaily
  Had our baggage overhauled;
Climbed the rocks to gather flowers
  Over which the vines had crawled.

Bought we shamrock by the handful,
  Took we carriages for Cork,
Where we spent some hours in resting,
  Not caring for a walk
In the rain which had continued
  All the blessed morning through,
As if in green old Ireland
  It had nothing else to do.

Hours later when the sky was clear,
  Took we carriages again
To St. Fionn Bar's grand cathedral,
  Which must have racked the brain

Of some of the old architects,
  Who planned that massive pile
Of masonry and stone work,
  In that far-off ancient style.

Through the country drove we after
  To Blarney Castle, by the way,
Where we viewed with breath abated,
  That grand ruin in decay;
Climbed the tower to its summit,
  Kissed the famous " Blarney Stone,"
Descended to its dungeons
  Of which little now is known.

Next the regions of Killarney
  On our programme did appear,
Took we train for Muckross Station,
  Landing there with little fear,
Stopped at the " Hotel Muckross,"
  Near the Abbey of that name,
A grand and stately ruin,
  Making Blarney rather tame.

The jaunting cars were taken,
  As the sun sank down to rest,
By numbers of our party,
  Their easy qualities to test;
But they styled them very funny
  Little wagons for a ride,
Pronouncing them not quite the thing
  For all sitting on one side.

—   --

The Sabbath morning broke at last
    With many a golden beam,
Making mountain-chain and lakelet
    Like a poem or a dream;
Gilding ruined Muckross Abbey
    With a glory half divine,
Peeping through the broken casements
    Where the ivies lightly twine.

To church we wandered slowly,
    On the morning of that day.
Drinking in the dewy perfume
    Of the flowers by the way;
Breathing air so cool, refreshing,
    Health-giving to us all,
Thinking, can this be old Ireland
    Over which hangs such a pall?

After church a drive was taken
    Through the Muckross grand estate,
Though we admired all its beauty,
    We pitied its sad fate,
To think of those broad acres,
    Of fields so green and fair,
Not paying for improvements
    Or keeping in repair.

Killarney, dear Killarney!
    Our memory clings to thee,
With your mountains rising grandly
    From the level of the sea,

Where among thy rocky caverns
  The eagle builds her nest,
While around thy sturdy bases
  The red deer shows his breast.

Next day from Muckross station
  Journeyed we for hours along,
Through scenery romantic,
  And with many a joke and song,
Fled the hours so swift and gaily,
  "Till at Dublin we arrived,
Thanking goodness we had reached there,
  And that all of us survived.

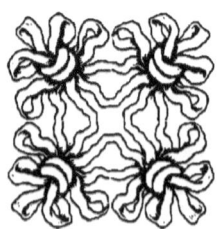

WALES.

HAT can I say of thee! of thy sea-bound shore!
Say thou art most lovely, just this and no more!
Or shall I repeat what others have said
In regard to thy mines, and thy deep iron bed?

No, I'll not mention these in this little tale,
Or tell any horror to make the cheek pale;
But just give in outline what we saw as we flew,
In the express that morning — then bid thee adieu.

Most romantic the views as we sped past thy bowers,
Of mountains and vales, of castles and towers,
With ruins most frowningly perched on the hill
By men of past ages, who built with much skill.

Suspended thy bridges far over our way,
Which shows the improvement of the present day;
With tunnels cut through the hillside so solid,
With comfortable homesteads but never one squalid.

13

Thy fields are well tended, thy flocks and thy fold
Are watched o'er by Shepherds, as they watched them of old.
Thy land seemed productive of comfort and gain,
Well cared for and governed in the present reign.

O could we have lingered on thy sea-girted shore,
Gone bathing and fishing and found out the store
Of knowledge, so precious, to fill up the mind,
And give pleasing thoughts as we left thee behind.

But our stay was too short to find out the story
Of historic honors—of battles and glory,
So with hearts full of pleasure at viewing thy beauties,
We flew on to England, to our increase of duties.

ENGLAND.

AT last we stood on English soil,
   And many did agree
There was less of pleasure than of toil
   In crossing the Irish sea.

But the ill effects were lessened,
   As we thought of all we'd seen,
As on to Chester we hastened,
   For Wales had lain between.

In Chester we spent one night,
   Stopping at "Queen Hotel,"
Where all seemed cheerful and bright,
   And where we soon felt well.

Then, taking carriage or 'bus,
   We drove around the city,
Viewing the quaint and curious,
   Seeing some things so pretty.

Next morn we arose at six o'clock
   And proceeded on our way
To Kenilworth Castle, a brick block,
   House of Leicester in decay.

Viewed these ruins, walked around,
   Hearing legends of the past;
Then hurried o'er the ground
   As the rain was falling fast.

15

Next to Warwick was the order,
  And to Warwick we did go,
Where we walked along its border,
  Saw the Avon's gentle flow—

Viewed the house and grounds outside,
  The old draw-bridge and the moat,
In which all of us took pride,
  As down its history we wrote.

The grounds were full of beauty
  With flower and shrub and tree,
And we praised them as our duty,
  Yes, praised them heartily.

We visited the "Warwick Vase"
  Of which so much is said;
Heard legends of a now past race,
  All of them being dead.

We were shown the interior
  Of the castle, full of art,
Long suites of rooms superior,
  In which Kings had taken part.

Saw where Queen Anne had slept,
  And Queen Victoria too,
And perhaps where oft' they'd wept
  At things they had to do.

Many, many rooms were looked through
  Where lovely things were seen;
Inlaid tables, rich in gold and blue,
  Walls hung with golden sheen.

Then to Stratford drove we slowly
  Through the rain in waterproof;
Bearing the discomforts lowly,
  But all wishing for a roof.

Stratford-on-Avon is the place
  Where Wm. Shakespeare was born;
We saw the tombs of all the race
  Of Shakespeares, on that morn.

Went through the church, and all around
  The grounds surrounding it;
Where Shakespeare was so often found,
  Where often he would sit.

We bought the famous Shakespeare spoon,
  And many a thing beside;
Took dinner in the afternoon,
  Then proceeded with our ride.

The country through which we drove that day
  Was beautiful and fine;
And as we drove along the way
  We wished for bright sunshine.

Arrived at Leamington town,
    We took train for Euston station,
And very soon were all set down
    In London, Pride of the Nation.

London by night was grand to see,
    With its rows on rows of light;
With crowds of folk so merrily
    Going ever to the right.

Our first day in town was rather wet
    And spent in looking 'round;
Talking and laughing with those we met
    Or riding under ground.

To "Chrystal Palace" late that day
    We took the Rail-way train,
And there we found a grand display
    Of things for making gain.

And other things we found beside
    Under that roof of glass,
In which the English take much pride,
    In which they do surpass.

Of statues old there was no lack;
    Of pictures too, so many;
And every kind of Bric-à-brac,
    Some selling for a penny.

The grounds, how shall I picture them?
With their Lakes and Islands too;
With statues of women and men,
Other attractions not a few.

We all attended a fine play
Of Trapeze, and slight of hand,
In which the actors gently sway
As they rise and fall or stand.

And many other things we saw
Before the close of day,
Delightful, and without a flaw
To take their charm away.

As eve approached the sky grew clear
And brilliant the display
Of fireworks, which did then appear
In colors bright and gay.

Thirty pieces or more, I'm sure,
Were thrown up in the air;
Causing the very most demure
To exclaim, "How very rare!"

For never had we seen a sight
So brilliant in its way; —
Two figures dancing in the light
To, "Ta-ra-ra-boom-de-aye."

And other pieces very grand,
  Arranged to music too;
With lovely music by the band,
  Home pieces old and new.

But now I'll leave this charming theme
  And return to London town,
Where we did rest, too tired to dream,
  That night on beds of *down*.

London next day, how charming!
  And through the fog we went
Shopping all the morning;
  On buying we were bent.

The afternoon and evening too
  Was full of interest,
For every hour we saw things new
  And each we thought the best.

Next morn was clear with bright sun-beam
  We drove, I scarce know where;
Seeing so much 'twas as a dream,
  Most beautiful and fair.

Saw White Chapel and Aldersgate;
  Also the Jewish Quarter;
The church where Milton lies in state,
  And Prince of Wales' daughter.

Westminster Abbey was gone through,
    Where, in a niche in wall,
Longfellow's bust shone bright and new,
    Seemingly to smile on all.

This Abbey is a structure rare
    Of which so much is read,
I need not an excuse declare
    For the little I have said.

I never can describe or name
    All we saw as we drew nigh
The towers and churches of past fame,
    Where forms of great men lie.

We saw the Palace of the Queen,
    Albert's Memorial Tower;
Also her jewels too were seen,
    We almost *felt* her power.

Saw largest hotel in the world,
    The " Hotel Metropole,"
Saw armories with flags unfurled,
    Armor and printed scroll.

Crossed London Bridge and rode along
    The " Row" and " St. James' Park,"
Hearing much of right and wrong,
    And reached hotel at dark.

And so the five whole days were spent
    Which were allowed us here,
Doing as each one's mind was bent;
    In the evening did appear—

Going to Theatre, Opera House,
    Or staying at home at will;
Some thought the day about enough
    For any one to fill.

And now the last hour did approach;
    We needs must haste away,
To New Haven sped in railway-coach,
    Early upon that day.

Farewell, farewell to England's shore,
    Thou lovely prosperous land;
Perhaps thou wilt be seen no more
    By the little "Ackley Band."

FRANCE.

DIEPPE! yes at last we were on the French shore,
Feeling happy to think we should cross channels
no more;
But wander around through this beautiful land,
See wonderful things and our knowledge expand.

From steamboat to train we all soon had changed,
With luggage secured and all things arranged,
After buying some fruit and looking around
At the Chalk-Cliffs, we rattled along o'er the ground.

The ride from Dieppe to Paris was fine
And, had we been favored with brighter sunshine,
I don't know how beautiful France would have seemed,
As we rode through the towns where busy life teemed.

Of these towns which we passed, very much could be said,
But no doubt of their history many have read,
So passing them by, we sped on our way
That we might be in Paris by close of the day.

23

Rouen! how that name will sad memories awake,
When we think of Joan who was burnt at the stake!
But as her sad story has often been told,
To you a more pleasing one I will unfold.

There were many fine towns scattered close by the Seine,
And through which we traveled that day in the train,
The country was lovely, so brilliant and gay,
With fields of bright colors all along the way.

As evening approached we at Paris arrived,
That wonderful Paris so often described;
And sure my poor pen can never write down
All we saw as we drove through that beautiful town.

Our kind guide, Mr. Vickers, a fine man by the way,
Soon had us through Customs without much delay,
Then seated in cabs we drove quickly along
Through all that wonderful, gaily-dressed throng.

Soon arrived at hotel the "Central" by name,
A hotel quite new, not connected with fame
We were shown our apartments, allowed a short rest,
And then sought the dining hall, our dinner in quest.

Next morn we arose much refreshed by our naps,
Dressed ready for driving, and with no mishaps,
Took cabs at the door and drove miles away
Through Paris and environs, on that long summer's day.

What did we see as we drove slowly along?
Saw gaily dressed folk going by with the throng;
Saw the "Louvre" and the Church of the Madeleine,
Largest in Paris, very handsome and plain.

Where Marie Antoinette and many had died
By terrible deaths, as is known far and wide;
Saw "Arc-de-Triomphe" whose height is immense,
Built by Napoleon I, a man of sound sense.

His original plan was to have built four
Of arches, in memory of victories a score,
But never but one reached completion, I'm told,
And this is Triomphe that stands out so bold.

Saw "Spiral Tower;" "Trocadéro," a very large dome,
Not as large as St. Peters seen later in Rome;
Large concert-hall too, and much more 'twas grand
We saw while in Paris, queen of the land.

"Jardin-des-Plants" with sweet flowers so gay,
Where all through the summer the visitors stray;
"Eiffel Tower," reaching upward its peak toward the sky,
The one tower in Europe that was e'er built so high.

Admiralty Square, Bridge Hill from old Bastile;
The Gobelin Manufactory where we saw a great pile
Of rugs, and lovely carpets of patterns intricate,
Made by men whose daily earnings are very moderate.

The " Palais-de-Justice" on the Isle-de-la-cité,
Was oft destroyed by fire which seemed such a pity;
The tomb of Napoleon; Corn Exchange and Market
Square.
Saw groups of scattered soldiers and heard music sweet
and rare.

Thus our first day in Paris sped swiftly along,
In the evening went to Opera or Theatre with the throng,
Some staying at the hotel where they rested for the night,
So as to be up early looking cheerful, glad and bright.

The second day in Paris we did just as we pleased,
Going shopping at Au-bon-Maché, or if the fancy seized,
Took drive around the city seeing many sights so new,
Buying souvenirs and *nick nacks* in numbers not a few.

Our third day was pleasant as to weather, which was fine,
In open cabs we started, soon had crossed the Paris line.
In the old town of Bois-de-Boulogne six miles away,
Seeing "Chateau of St. Cloud" and Grand Trianon by the
way.

The "Chateau of St. Cloud" has a history of its own,
But as the space is limited it cannot here be shown ;
So has the " Grand Trianon" built long years ago,
By Louis XIV for Marie-de-Mainteno.'

Sweet gardens, and state carriages were looked at on that
    day;
Galleries of awful paintings of great battles in array;
Statue of Napoleon who was Emperor of France
Heard histories and legends which their value did enhance.

Our guides were kind, the weather fine, and everything so
    bright;
We enjoyed ourselves exceedingly 'till the closing in of
    night.
Then we went to our hotel for dinner and to rest,
To prepare for the evening of social talk and jest.

Next day was ours, to go or stay as inclination willed,
As eve approached we all declared the day was more than
    filled,
For shopping at Au-bon-Machè, and other places too,
Was in itself a hard day's work as one would wish to do.

And so each day of all the six was filled up in its way,
Some going to church on Sunday others to Louvre did
    stray.
The "Louvre" has many rare old things and statues old
    and new
"Venus-de-Milo," an old Greek piece and a thousand
    others too.

Sunday, being our last day in Paris, we were told
To pack our trunk and ready make for a journey long and
   cold.
We rode by rail that night and day for more than sixteen
   hours,
Through dark and damp (with lighted lamp) past many
   lovely bowers.

This closed our stay in Paris, most lovely in the world,
And many a sigh we breathed that night as along the way
   we whirled,
But sighs nor tears will ne'er avail, I'll tell you the reason
   why —
To everything thats' fair in life we have to say "good bye."

ITALY.

ITALY, thou fairest of lands,
  Land of poetry and song!
How shall I ever describe thee,
  With-out doing thee wrong?
How shall I tell of the wonders
  Seen on thy beautiful shore?
How describe things of past ages,
  Things of historical lore?

Turin was the city selected
  For us to stop in one night.
We landed mid dust and confusion,
  Our faces and clothes in a plight,
For tunnels in numbers we'd passed through,
  As through the Alp region we came;
But the scenes had been grand and romantic;
  Paying for discomforts, I claim.

In this city we saw much to please us,
  Took drive or a walk all around,
Stopped at the hotel, "The Feder,"
  An old building which covers much ground.

29

In this house the floors are of marble,
    Inlaid in different design;
And the stairs, self-supporting,
    Give them an easy incline.

From Turin to Genoa, we traveled
    In Railway-carriage, next day,
Arriving in time for our dinner
    At " Hotel Central " by way.
Then in open carriage, provided,
    And through the brightest sunshine,
We drove through this ancient city,
    To see things substantial and fine.

Saw Cathedral of Annunciation,
    St. John's tomb by the way,
In which now his ashes are resting,
    'Till the Resurrection Day.
Picture of Naggolo Paginni,
    The great violinist, was seen
His violin resting in proof safe
    From fire, to protect it they mean.

Church of " St. Lorenzo " was looked through;
    Built hundreds of years ago;
Then to " Campo Santo " hastened,
    Where we saw tombs in a row;
Most wonderful sculpturing also,
    Fashioned by a master hand,
Of monuments, tablets, and scroll-work,
    Most beautiful work in the land.

The day was most perfect with sunlight,
   The arch of the sky was so clear;
The view of the Alps from the city
   With soft fleecy clouds did appear.
The air was delicious, refreshing,
   Tempered with breezes so mild
Which blew from the great gulf of Genoa,
   And almost our senses beguiled.

The city of Genoa is noted
   For its historic events;
Here was the birth-place of Columbus,
   A man of learning and sense.
It also has two fortifications,
   Which enclose it around;
The only city in Europe,
   Where two rows of fortress' are found.

At night we left Genoa for Pisa,
   By rail-way passing along
Through beautiful scenery and grove-shade,
   Amid much laughter and song.
The twilight was long in its closing,
   Which gave a fine view, as we passed,
Of the beautiful Medeterranean,
   A sea whose blue waters are vast.

Through tunnels we passed in succession,
   Which gave us much fun in their way,
As to close the window each minute,
   Was quite a hard task, I may say.

31

But the night was so cool and refreshing,
    We did not such labor find;
Sweet fruits and candies passed often,
    While stories relieved the mind.

Pisa was reached about midnight,
    Then we took cabs for the "Grand,"
'Tis an old palace converted
    Into hotel, understand.
This house is built near to the "Arno,"
    A river of some renown;
The city of ancient construction,
    Two thousand year old town.

Next morn we arose and proceeded
    In cabs, to the "Leaning Tower;"
Then visited a grand old Cathedral,
    Where we spent more than an hour.
St. John's Baptistery connected
    With this fine church was gone through,
Where was a whispering gallery,
    Which gave many echoes, so true.

In this grand old church there was service
    Going on as we entered that day:
The organ was giving sweet music,
    While people came in there to pray.
We examined the paintings and altars
    The lamp made by Galileo,
A wonderful ancient construction,
    Made many years ago.

Through graveyard we wandered that morning
   Seeing the old cypress tree,
Walking on ground that was holy,
   From Palestine over the sea;
Then to hotel all returning,
   Through the lovely sunshine,
We, a small trade did engage in,
   Of pieces of marble, so fine.

At night we left Pisa for Roma,
   Arriving near the midnight hour;
Stopped at "Grand Hotel de Russie,"
   Whose grounds were a beautiful bower —
Of orange, and lemon, and plum tree,
   With statues and fountains behind,
Flowers and shrubs intermingled,
   Retreat sweet and cool, all combined.

The paths of the gardens were graveled,
   With pebbles so fine and so white,
They shone through the bright summer darkness,
   Like ribbons of silvery light.
The statues gleamed white through the gloaming,
   The fountains made musical sound,
Causing the senses to wonder,
   If that was a " Paradise found."

There in that lovely old Roma,
   Of which so many have read,
We rested for six days and over
   Seeing the living and dead;

Walking where Christs own apostles,
    And even His saints did appear,
Seeing the tombs of old martyrs,
    Who died for their Lord without fear.

Our first day in Rome was most quiet,
    The weather so warm at mid-day,
'Twas thought best not then to venture
    From the hotel far away;
Thus some were contented to wander,
    Or sit in the Edenly bower,
Keep cool and eat fruit until evening,
    Then the young people danced for an hour.

Next morning was hot with bright sunshine,
    But that did not our courage daunt,
No, we were all ready in carriage,
    Prepared for a long mornings jaunt,
To " Pincian Hill" drove we slowly,
    (Not one of the seven in Rome,)
And from its top viewed the city,
    For that we had many miles come.

Next to " Palatine Hill" we proceeded,
    Which *is* one of the seven,
There we walked among ruins,
    Hearing their history given;
Hearing the legend and story,
    Of a race which lived long ago,
Who those old ruins did inhabit,
    As our kind guide tried to show.

To the Capitol next was the order,
    And we on to the Capitol came,
Drinking there from a fountain of water,
    Erected in somebody's name.
In this house saw many old relics,
    Of statues no end in a line,
"Mars" being the largest among them,
    An old Grecian piece, very fine.

Saw skeletons there of great ladies,
    Of men who had died in their prime,
Heard stories about the past ages,
    Almost from begining of time.
Next drove through the streets of the city,
    Seeing each minute things new,
So much we were almost distracted,
    With that ever varying view.

At mid-day we rested at hotel,
    After which we took carriage again,
And drove to the "Church of All Angels"
    There for some time to remain;
Michael Angelo was the founder,
    Of this church as is well known
To all readers of foreign travel,
    And to those to whom it is shown.

"St. Sebastian's," next on the programme,
    Another church of much fame,
Where his Effigy, pierced by the arrows,
    Lies resting "In His Name."

35

Next "St. John's Church" was looked through
  And its chapels also,
Where we heard beautiful music,
  From organ, so sweet and low.

In "St. John's Church," twelve apostles
  All in white marble are cast,
Standing in niches so gravely,
  Reminding us all of the past.
Still another the "St. Mary,"
  A magnificent church in its way,
Where is kept part of the manger,
  In which the infant Christ lay.

"St. Peter in Chains" was examined
  Where we saw the old chain,
Said to be worn by St. Peter,
  While he in prison had lain;
Next "Santa Maria Maggiore,"
  A very old church was gone through,
There we saw frieze in mosaic,
  Of pictures most beautiful too.

And one other place I must mention,
  That we saw upon that day, —
A small building near to "St. John's"
  Where people gather to pray.
They ascend on their knees many stairs,
  Made of marble so white,
Said to be from the house of Pilate,
  Walked over by Jesus of light.

Next, through the city drove slowly,
  Along past Palatine Hill,
Going to Catacombs after,
  And such a large space as they fill;
Under the earth is this grave-yard,
  Extending for many a mile
Sebastian's tomb at its entrance,
  Then thousands of many a style.

We passed the old "Colosseum,"
  Now in a ruinous state,
It covers a large space in Roma,
  Decay is its ultimate fate.
And many fine orchards we passed by
  Of peaches, figs, lemons and such,
Arriving at hotel near evening,
  Then our dinner enjoyed very much.

In the morn we took open carriage,
  And drove through modern Rome,
Seeing many new and old objects,
  Some not unlike those at home.
Next to the "Mamertine Prison,"
  Down in the vaults we did go,
Where Peter and Paul were imprisoned
  In the harsh reign of Nero —

Then the four chapels connected,
  With this old prison were seen,
But into one only we ventured,
  As into so many we'd been:

Next to the "Forum" drove slowly,
  Through the heat of a summer's morn,
Heard much about Julius Cæsar,
  And events before we were born.

Then the "Vatican" claimed our attention,
  And there too a story we heard;
Next to "St. Peter's" we hastened,
  Heard its history word for word;
This church is a wonderful structure
  Of most ancient and delicate art,
Many hundreds have spent there a life-time
  Preparing their difficult part.

"St. Peters!" how shall I describe it,
  Or give a faint idea to you,
Of its great beauty and grandeur?—
  This is a task for the few.
I can tell of its wonderful altar,
  Inlaid with pearl of great price,
And so exquisitely fashioned,
  As to look like embroidery, nice:—

Then the cherubims and the infants,
  Made of marble so white,
And looking like beautiful angels,
  Just from the realms of light;
And the magnificent paintings
  By Raphael, of many a saint,
Ah! he was an artist to follow,
  For he a grand picture could paint.

This church is the finest in Europe,
    Or perhaps in the world that appears,
Its chapels, its frescoes, and art work
    Have cost thousands on thousands for years.
Much time could be spent in description
    Of this beautiful church built in Rome;
But on to the end I must hasten,
    Not even describing its dome.

After seeing this church we took luncheon
    At a café by the way,
And shopped for an hour or two after,
    Buying bright sashes so gay,
Souvenir spoons and bright jewels,
    Trifles for loved ones at home,
Knowing well such would be pleasing,
    If brought from that lovely old Rome.

That evening we went out in parties
    To a most popular square,
To listen to best band in Roma,
    To see all 'twas lovely and fair.
Rome that night was most brilliant,
    ('Tis often the case of an eve,)
In the square were set little tables,
    Where things were sold, I believe.

The band played many selections,
    The soldiers walked to and fro,
The young sat around with the matrons,
    In seats placed row upon row,

Or strolled up and down with their lovers,
  Or together ate ices so sweet,
Most of the maidens were lovely,
  All dressed very pretty and neat.

The next day, being Sunday, we rested,
  The weather so hot at mid-day,
'Twas thought best not far to venture,
  But close to the hotel to stay;
Yet some of the " Pilgrims" then hastened
  To church, on that morning so fair,
Feeling perhaps 'twas their one chance
  To see devout Romans at prayer.

Monday, a long day of leisure,
  We all did just as we pleased,
Going to "St. Peter's" or elsewhere;
  Or, such opportunity seized,
Of visiting old or new places,
  Shopping for things of the past,
Seeing new sights in old Roma,
  Regretting that day was our last.

Next day we left Roma for Naples,
  And rode by rail many miles
Seeing, as we passed through the country,
  Many old ruinous piles.
Seeing the Acqueducts also,
  Through which the clean waters flow
Supplying with moisture the city,
  Which is built some miles below.

The view all the way was so pleasing,
　　The day so delightfully bright,
We enjoyed very much our long journey,
　　Arriving at Naples near night:
Stopped at a beautiful hotel,
　　The " Hotel Royal" by name,
Which faces the broad bay of Naples,
　　That beautiful bay of wide fame.

Naples is a very large city,
　　With hundreds of thousands of lives
Massed together in limited quarters,
　　Almost like bees in their hives;
But the city itself is delightful,
　　Washed ever by waves of the bay,
While "Vesuvius" watches beside it,
　　Whose summit is not far away.

On arriving at Naples that evening,
　　Some took carriage and drove through the town,
To see the old tomb of " Virgel,"
　　And other old things of renown.
The night was most perfect with moon-light,
　　The bay like a large looking-glass,
With different objects reflected,
　　Causing a wierd looking mass.

The air was both cool and refreshing,
　　As it blew from the water so clear,
The view of the city resplendent,
　　With thousands of lights did appear.

We all took a walk on that evening,
　　Going shopping to lovely Arcade,
Buying spoons and other small trifles,
　　Returning along the Parade.

In the morning took steamer at Naples
　　Sailing across its wide bay,
To Sorrento, not many miles distant,
　　A very fine town in its way;
The sail, from Naples to Sorrento,
　　Occupied nearly three hours,
Some of the passengers sea-sick,
　　The weather threatening showers.

Most of us got off at Sorrento,
　　Taking small boats to the land;
While others went on to "Capri,"
　　An Island by gentle winds fanned;
And some thought to see the "Blue Grotto,"
　　But soon they found out their mistake
As the guide had told them at starting,
　　They could not an entrance make.

At Sorento we found all so lovely,
　　We did not regret in the least,
That we had forgone the great pleasure
　　Of Capri's and Blue Grotto's feast.
For there the gardens were blooming,
　　Which surrounded hotel,
With every kind of sweet flower,
　　With shrub and fruit tree as well.

Our hotel was named the "Victoria,"
　　And stood on a bluff high and free,
Overlooking the Gulf of Sorrento,
　　And Mediterranean sea;
The house in itself was a picture,
　　Our rooms were so pleasant and neat,
We were delighted to stop there,
　　In that most charming retreat.

After luncheon we all did assemble,
　　Took carriage and drove through the town,
Past beautiful gardens and vineyards,
　　Whose vines with rich fruits were bent down;
The day now brightened with sunshine,
　　The air, not too warm or too cold,
Blew from the mountains so gently,
　　While Vesuvius smoked as of old.

Around the walled drive drove we slowly,
　　The loveliest one in the world,
On one side the mountains above us,
　　Had clouds from Vesuvius hurled,
On the other the sea washed the shore,
　　Making soft musical sound;
Small beggars ran after the carriage,
　　For pennies we threw on the ground.

Twenty miles was the length of the journey
　　That we had driven that day,
Enjoying each moment more fully,
　　The beautiful scenes by the way;

In the eve we returned to the hotel,
    Next we repaired to a hall,
Where we saw natives dancing
    In costumes like fancy ball.

Heard music by band from Sorrento,
    The very best in the town,
Then songs in Italian were rendered
    By a very comical clown;
There were several more variations,
    To vary the sports of the eve,
Such as small feats by the dancers,
    Which much applause did receive.

Then a collection was taken,
    Which the festivities closed,
Then we retired to our chambers,
    Where for some hours we reposed,
Dreaming perhaps of our dear ones,
    Thousands of miles away,
Or perhaps of our trip on the morrow,
    To the ruins of Pompeii.

The following morn we took carriage
    And drove through Sorrento again,
Seeing new sights by the way-side,
    Sights both for laughter and pain;
Passing by many a home-stead,
    Where poverty ruled quite supreme,
And passing the rich man's dominion,
    Whose lands were as bright as a dream,

44

With beautiful groves of fruit trees,
    Where the green olive's hung,
Together with lemons and almonds,
    And grapes to the lattices clung.
The gardens were full of choice flowers
    Almost of tropical growth.
While, among all this beauty, were gleaming
    Fountains and statues of worth.

Near noon we arrived at Pompeii,
    And stopped at a small hotel,
Where we took luncheon and rested,
    Bought pictures and things there to sell;
Then to the ruins proceeded,
    Closely following our guide,
Walking through fierce burning sunshine,
    Up many a steep hill-side.

Ah, the ruins! how shall I describe them,
    As we saw them standing so still?
As they have stood for many ages?
    Why 'twould a small volume fill!
We walked through the old " House of Sallust,"
    We sat in the bath-room awhile,
There we had fine pictures taken,
    Sitting on an old ruined pile.

We listened to guide while he told us,
    Of how Pompaii was destroyed,
Made notes of the dates and the figures,
    Thus all our time was employed,

'Till getting quite tired of the sameness
    Of story of this house and that,
We gathered in an old Amphitheatre;
    And down for a few minutes sat.

Then a silence fell over the party,
    Our thoughts, going back to the time
When Pompeii was not a lost ruin,
    But a flourishing town in its prime;
Where men worshiped idols of marble,
    Having gods all standing around
In the streets, and in private dwellings,—
    Some ruins to this day are found.

After stopping by fountain of Flora,
    Walking through many a street,
We left the ruins of Pompeii,
    Whose story's too sad to repeat;
Left them to time and its changes,
    Left them to crumble away,
Until in some future ages,
    They'll be in hopeless decay.

Next the Museum was looked through,
    Where we saw so many things,
Taken from out the lost ruins,
    Bread, nuts, coffee, and strings,
Skeletons, bones of lost beings,
    Who died in the great over-throw,
And were burried by masses of ashes,
    Hundreds of years ago.   .

As we drove from Pompeii near the evening
    We looked at the hills which surround
That once beautiful prosperous valley,
    Where everything rich could be found,
At Vesuvius which caused all the trouble,
    And wondered if at some future date,
There would be such an awful eruption,
    As that which settled Pompeii's fate.

Some of the young men of the party
    Engaged a few horses and guide,
To make the ascent of Vesuvius,
    Climbing slowly up on one side,
Going there to look into the crater,
    Where a bright fire can be seen,
Walking over very hot places,
    Where *few* of the many have been.

The rest of us saw Herculaneum,
    Which is a lost city also,
Destroyed the same as Pompeii,
    By Vesuvius' past over-flow;
This ruin still lies under ground,
    To which we had to descend,
With lighted tapers before us,
    And such a weird light as they lend.

This closed our long day of sight-seeing,
    And we were all glad to sit down
In carriage, until we reached Naples,
    That lovely old Italian town.

On the way we had quite a diversion
   All the horses being tired out,
Some five of them fell in succession,
   Causing a most lively rout.

But at last we were all landed
   At "Hotel Royal" again,
After a day most exciting,
   Well mixed with pleasure and pain.
That night our dreams were quite troubled
   With things we had seen through the day;
Or Vesuvious in grand eruption,
   Destroying long lost Pompeii.

Next morn we left Naples for Roma,
   Rode many miles in the train,
Through a new part of the country,
   Past many fields of ripe grain;
The way through the Appenine region
   Was pleasant, but rather too warm,
Saw fields under good cultivation,
   Forming many a farm.

At Rome we stopped only for luncheon,
   Then to Florence we came
Stopped at "Grand Hotel de Florence,"
   Where we soon wrote our name.
There we found things as they should be,
   Very neat, pleasant and cool,
There we stopped over Sunday,
   As in the course was the rule.

'Twas nine-thirty o'clock in the evening,
    When we were set down at hotel,
And after a light tea was served us,
    Then to rooms and soon to sleep fell.
Next morn we arose quite refreshéd,
    Took carriage and drove through the town,
Seeing churches and other fine buildings
    With exteriors moss-grown and brown.

First the church of "Santa Croce,"
    Where Micheal Angelo is laid,
And where is Dantes' Memorial,—
    He was born in Florence, 'tis said.
Statues of great men were looked at
    Pictures and sculpturing too,
Chapels that cost many fortunes,
    To carry successfully through.

Santa Croce is not yet completed,
    Men were there laying the floor
Of marbles and lovely mosaics,
    Which will last ages and more.
These marbles are polished so highly,
    That all is reflected again,
Even the dome with its pictures,
    Is in them repeated so plain.

Next gallery full of fine paintings,
    Which represent schools of art;
The name of the artist on picture,
    In which he has taken a part.

Next came a room full of statues,
　Adonis, Satyr, Dancing Faun,
With a hundred of others beside them,
　Seen on that memorable morn.

Then the King's palace was gone through,
　Where many fine paintings were seen;
Furniture of best manufacture,
　With elegant curtains between.
The Arno was crossed through the palace
　Where a gallery on either side
Was hung with beautiful pictures,
　In which the king takes much pride.

After seeing so much in the art line,
　We shopped a little for change,
At restaurant taking our luncheon,
　Where we had fun *making* change.
Next we returned to the hotel,
　Where *I* thought better to stay,
But the others went sight-seeing after,
　As if it was nothing but play.

Next, Sunday came to our relief,
　When some of us could rest,
But many went out just the same,
　Liking constant motion best.
There being no English church in town,
　Some to other churches strayed;
Or took a walk, or drive, around,
　While other people prayed.

That night we heard the order,
　　From our respected guide,
That we must rise at four o'clock,
　　To take an early ride;—
About ten hours in length 'twould be
　　Reaching Venice in afternoon,
With many a sigh we said good bye,
　　Retiring very soon.

Next morn at the appointed hour,
　　We met in dining-hall,
Taking breakfast rather hastily,
　　All answering to the call
From our guide, that we were ready,
　　And soon were on the way,
Passing through much lovely country,
　　And (fifty) tunnels on that day.

Many towns we passed or entered,
　　Where was much to interest,
Balogna, one of the many,
　　And where we did invest
In sausage, of the same name,
　　Which tasted very good,
With hard-bread of the country,
　　Which seemed the staple food.

At last we saw fair Venice,
　　And soon were sailing round
In gondola, rowed by gondolier,
　　Through grand canal or sound:

Soon arrived at end of journey
  And at hotel were set down,
The name the "Grand et New York,"
  One of the best in town.

Venice, can I ever describe
  This city of the sea?
Give an idea of its beauty,
  Or of its community?
Of what we saw in sailing round
  Through its many streets?
Or walking on the little ground
  Where are found some quiet retreats?

After resting for an hour,
  Took gondola's at the door,
And went to see the finest lace,
  Hand made by the poor.
After buying what we needed,
  And looking through the rooms,
We proceeded to the churches,
  Where we saw many tombs.

"Church of the Frair," a fine edifice,
  Was beautiful indeed,
Decorated by its wealthy patrons,
  Who have done a kindly deed,
As in all the churches we had seen,
  Was much wealth and labor spent,
To make them last for ages,—
  On that the mind seemed bent.

Now the evening hour approached,
    When we back to hotel sailed,
Seeing interesting objects,
    Before the twilight paled;
Seeing " House of Desdemona "
    The " Browning Palace," too,
Passing under " Bridge of Sighs,"
    By many a pleasing view.

That eve was lovely as a dream,
    With moon so round and full,
Casting shadows o'er the waters,
    Making picture of the whole
Lighting up the black gondola's
    With their solitary light,
Bringing out the lovely city,
    Making all so clear and bright.

Some found friends in that fair city,
    Which was a glad surprise
Making time pass off so quickly,
    As home subjects did arise,
As question followed question,
    And answer followed fast,
The evening dropped into space,
    And good-nights were said at last.

Next day we went on foot around
    Through Venice's lovely square,
It being said that in Europe
    There is none that can compare,

And surely 'tis a lovely spot
　Where many doves are fed;
Enclosed around on every side,
　By houses white and red.

"St. Marks" stands at one side,
　A church, so very old,
Commencèd in eighth century,
　Not yet fiinished, we were told,
Inside 'tis truly splendid,
　With columns set with stone
Most precious, brought from countries
　Of which little then was known.

Its bell-tower and its clock-tower,
　Detached from church stand free;
The clock tower has a queer old face,
　Which has a history;
Two images of Moors at top,
　With hammers strike the hour,
The legend runs that a man once hit
　Was knocked dead upon that tower.

Much more of that church could be said,
　But time nor space admit,
With regret at not doing it justice,
　I on to the next place flit.
At a well in a court or square,
　We drank the water pure,
Drawn by a woman of Venice,
　Whose face looked quite demure.

The "Doge's Palace" next I think,
    A grand building in its way
With rooms hung full of paintings,
    Something awful the display.
One of our "Lord in Hades,"
    And one the "Judgment Seat,"
One the largest in the world,
    Whose painting was a feat.

We passed from room to gallery,
    Hung with tapestries so fine,
Through Council Chamber also,
    And through doors red like wine.
Made from Cedar-tree of "Lebanan,"
    From Constantinople brought,
Which must have cost a figure,
    And required much time and thought.

That eve we sat on veranda
    And listened to a band .
Stationed in a large gondola,
    Which was gailey manned
With young men and fair misses,
    Who guitars and banjos played,
Or sang some lovely songs,
    For the "Pilgrims'" serenade.

Next morn we left fair Venice,
    And on to Milan came,
Seeing many lovely villages,
    And towns of ancient fame;

Saw the old town of "Verona"
  From which Shakespeare wrote his play,
"Two Gentlemen of Verona,"
  And others, by the way.

Saw the Alps in all their grandeur,
  And a lake of some renown;
We sped swiftly through the country,
  'Til at last we were set down
In station, at our journey's end,
  And very glad were we, —
Took crrriage, and drove quickly
  A Cathedral grand, to see.

That Cathedral was magnificent
  And is noted far and wide,
So I'll not go into detail,
  As I've other things beside
To mention, that we saw while there,
  And yet be very brief,
As my story's getting lengthy,
  The end will give relief.

The town itself is very large,
  Next to Naples in extent,
Its streets are wide, its shops are fine,
  And on shopping we were bent.
That eve we went from shop to shop,
  Buying spoons and other things;
The Arcade was very attractive,
  Where we bought the Milan rings.

As we retired that night to rest
  Our last on that bright shore,
We thought of the seventeen days w'ed spent,
  And wished there had been more;
But, like all the other countries,
  We had from thee to part,
No matter how much we love thee
  Nor how near it broke the heart.

Good-bye, most lovely Italy!
  I know I've fallen short,
Of giving a good description,
  But bright visions I have brought,
From your lovely sunny country,
  The fairest in the land,
Which has offered many pleasures,
  To the little " Ackley Band."

SWITZERLAND.

SUCH grandeur and such beauty, as that which met our view,
As from Milan we traveled and near the Alps we drew.
On either side, the mountains rose to a tremendous height,
O'er hung with craigs and boulders, oft obscuring all the light,

The lofty peaks with snow-capped tips, the valleys that we
passed,
The waterfalls and cataracts, flowing down their sides so fast;
All made a wondrous picture, which we never can forget,
It shall be ever treasured, and was left with much regret.

Much beauty and much grandeur, (things 'twere awful too,
we saw,)
As we entered many tunnels, frightful places these, to awe;
Or crossed a bridge so narrow over some dread abyss,
Where foamed a torrent loudly with seething, boiling hiss.

We passed many a lake and hamlet of historic note;
Homesteads nestled by the way-side, far from the world
remote,
Where men live in blissful ignorance of cities and their sin,
Surrounded by grand nature, whose mountains close them in.

But I never can describe the scenes we passed through
     on that day
Or give a faint idea of the beautiful display;
Of the ever changing views, so romantic and so grand,
Which we saw upon the morning that we entered Switzerland.

Near night we reached " Lucerne," full of beauty is that town,
Surrounded by the Alps, whose peaks rise white and brown ;
Where among their sturdy bases many lakes shine bright
     and clear,
And upon their lovely shores many villages appear.

We stopped at " Hotel Europe," in this most charming of
     retreats,
But only for a minute, then were hurrying through the streets,
Going to see the far famed Lion, hewn in the solid rock,
In memory of dead Swiss, a brave heroic stock.

Then to " Glacier Gardens " hastened, there to look around,
To see the marks of nature, which are in these gardens
     found ;
Being formed by many glaciers, of past ages slipping down
From the mountain-side afar, far above that lovely town.

Next morn we arose quite early, took carriage at the door,
And proceeded to the landing of the steamer near the shore,
Took boat across the lovely lake of Lucerne, upon that day,
Seeing many charming objects all along the way.

Up Mt. Rigi next we climbed along in observation car,
Seeing scenery so lovely, which the clouds would often mar,
As they rolled away below us, obscuring many a view,
Which was reflected with great splendor, where the sun
    had broken through.

At top we wandered round an hour, took dinner at hotel;
Seeing views from top of Rigi, of village and of dell;
Looking o'er the tops of mountains, seeing fields so green
    and fair;
Thinking there is nothing made by man, that with nature
    can compare.

Down the other side of Rigi we made the slow descent,
Seeing many views so charming, as along the way we went;
Of homestead or of hamlet, nestled close beside a hill;
And many caves, and water-falls, and rivers which they fill.

At foot of that grand mountain we took boat across "Lake
    Zug."
Where for an hour we halted in the little town of Zug,
Then on again we traveled, now in a rail-way train,
To the old town of Zurich, where we halted once again.

Stopped there for near two hours, and looked around the
    town,
Which had a pleasing history, and objects of renown.
Some took cabs and went exploring to see everything they
    could,
While others rested quietly in the station if they would.

Again we boarded train and to "Neuhausen" took our way,
Arriving at that charming place just at the close of day,
When the stars were all a-shining, while the dew was on the
    grass,
Saw the "Falls of the Rhine" illumined, and in beauty they
    surpass.

We stopped at the "Belle-vue," a fine hotel with fine grounds
Which overlooks the Falls, where the water ceaseless bounds
Makes sweet music while one wanders thro' the gardens
    down below,
Where many shrubs and flowers and fruit-trees also grow.

Next day was like the day before, most beautiful and bright,
We took a walk around the town, seeing many a pleasant
    sight,
Returning to our hotel we rested for an hour,
Then took our way to the station, leaving that delightful
    bower.

Adieu, fair Switzerland, adieu! we could no longer stay,
But must hasten on our journey, be in Germany that day ;
Where fine views and scenes awaited us and good cheer
    did abound,
But grandeur and sublimity in Switzerland had been found.

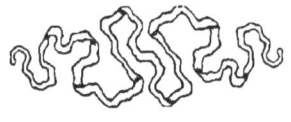

61

GERMANY.

AS I write of each new country,
   'Twas our happy lot to see,
I think of Him who made them all
   In such great variety.

Some bordered by the ocean,
   And some by mountain chain,
Others by them both combined,
   To strengthen their domain.

Still others where the land surrounds,
   With just a border line,
To protect them from their neighbor,
   Their province thus confine.

And in many of the countries
   Through which we passed along,
Men spoke a different language,
   Some as musical as song.

I noticed too, each Nation
   Was courteous and kind,
Ever ready to oblige us,
   If a pretext they could find.

Our ride that day was pleasant,
　As the scenery was new;
Passed many a lovely village,
　And many a charming view.

One town or village had a name,
　Which had a funny sound;
"Gottmadingen," as they spell it,
　Made a gentle laugh go round.

And other funny things we saw
　Upon that long, long ride,
As we passed through eleven tunnels,
　Along the Black Hills' side.

But we were getting used to tunnels,
　And rather liked the change
Of passing these dark places,
　Giving sunshine in exchange.

The "Black Forest" was dark indeed,
　Which was a mass of pine
Of thickest growth and under-brush,
　Where the sun can never shine.

The towns through which we passed along
　Looked thriving in their way;
The farms seemed quite productive
　Of vegetables and hay.

No walls nor fence divided them ;
　Each man, his patch of ground
Had planted with a different grain
　From the others which surround.

Saw women working in the fields,
　Along with men and boys ;
Contentment seemed their happy lot,
　Among those rural joys.

At last we reached our journey's end,
　" Baden Baden" just at night ;
Got off at Central station,—
　Next, our hotel came in sight.

"Stadt Baden " was the name of it
　And it near the station stands ;
There saw many soldiers marching,
　And heard music from brass bands.

That night went round the city,
　Which is a watering place,
Where people drink of the waters,
　For ills of the human race.

Next Sunday dawned upon us
　With sunshine bright and clear,
We went sightseeing on that morning
　To old ruined castle near.

Then we drank the pure spring-water,
  Of which so much was said;
Some went around to churches,
  Some stayed at home and read.

We saw the baths of Baden,
  Where people, in poor health,
Take baths to make them stronger;
  These are people of much wealth.

In the eve went to Casino,
  Which had an extensive ground,
And was lighted up by lanterns
  And gas-jets all around.

The scene was very brilliant,
  With fire-works in the air;
And many thousand people
  Walking through the lovely square.

We listened to fine music,
  Did a little shopping too,
And although it was the Sabbath,
  We had all that we could do.

Next morn we arose quite early,
  And proceeded on our way
To Heidleberg by rail-way train,
  Where we made a four hours' stay.

Took carriage to the ruin
  Of the castle of that name;—
A very extensive ruin,
  Putting those we'd seen to shame.

After hearing all the story
  Of this room and of that;
We went into the cellar,
  There saw the great wine vat.—

Which held fifty thousand gallons
  Of wine, in days of old,
When Kings and Queens held revels
  With the Knights and warriors bold.

The grounds were well examined,
  Which surround these ruins fine;
We walked through paths of beauty,
  O'er hung with flower and vine;

After which we took the journey
  On foot, across the city;
Buying souvenirs of Heidleberg
  And many views so pretty.

We took luncheon at the station
  Of fruits, cakes, and lager-beer;
Then on again toward " Worms,"
  We rode with usual cheer.

On the way saw much flat country
And factories of the best;
At "Athol" saw a German stork,
On a chimney taking rest.

Arrived at Worms at evening,
And there were soon set down
At the "Hartman" and the "Europe,"
Some of the best in town.

Next morn we arose at four o'clock,
And drove through that queer old town,
Seeing Martin Luther's monument,
And his statue, old and brown.

Then on to "Meyence" traveled,
Stopped there a little while,
Seeing many things of interest,
And many an ancient pile.

Took steam-boat at the landing,
Soon had left "Mayence" behind,
As we sailed adown the river;
'Tis the Rhine,— I have in mind.

On either side were lovely views
Of town, and village too,
With castles perched upon the hills,
And some of them quite new.

And many old and ruined piles,
　　Built hundreds of years ago ;
All having pleasing histories,
　　Which I hav'nt space to show.

Saw fair " Bingen," heard the story
　　Of the " Mouse Tower," on that day,
And other pretty legends,
　　Of old ruins in decay.

Saw the far famed town of " Bonn,"
　　Where Beethoven was born ;
And many, many vineyards,
　　From which rich wine is drawn.

The day was lovely, bright and clear,
　　And we from care so free,
We found the sail most pleasant,
　　Oft laughed with child-like glee.

We took dinner on the steamer,
　　Which tasted very good,
'Leven courses on the bill of fare,
　　Of different kinds of food.

Near night we reached Cologne,
　　A very ancient city,
Stopped at Hotel " Victoria,"
　　Where all was neat and pretty.

In the morning, all took carriage
    And drove from place to place,
Seeing things I can't describe,
    For lack of time and space.

I only a few can mention,
    And these the very best;
First, Church of St. Ursula,
    Where bones of martyrs rest.

That church was curious indeed,
    Just crowded full of bone,
Of many thousand vergins,
    Who had died there at Cologne.

Next to the great Cathedral
    Which was grand, magnificent!
And, like all the foreign churches
    Great sums had there been spent.

There saw the tomb of "Three wise men,"
    All made of solid gold,
And set around with precious stones,
    "To tempt the robber bold.

And there we saw grand paintings
    Of Madonna and of saint,
By artists of world-wide renown;—
    Grand pictures those to paint.

And many other things 'twere grand—
   In that old church were seen;
Not appreciated quite as much,
   As the first in which we'd been.

Next drove to the Museum,
   Saw Ruben's pictures there
And those painted by his pupils,
   Of many a scene so fair,

And scenes too that were awful,
   And many that were grand,
Of martyrs and fair women,
   Whose destruction had been planned.

After seeing all those paintings,
   So fine in every way,
We saw the lovely portrait
   Of Queen Louise that day.

No one can e'er describe that face,
   So beautiful, refined,
With figure of repose and grace;
   All these were there combined.

After spending all the morning,
   In such a pleasant way,
We shopped a little after,
   Then to hotel did stray,

Next prepared to leave the city,
    And soon were on the train,
Flying through much lovely country,
    Past many a field of grain,

And villages and hamlets,
    Across the country wide,
We sped along most swiftly,
    On that interesting ride.

Soon we had left fair Germany,
    And into Belgium ran,
Where our luggage was examined,
    By an official man.

O, Germany, fair Germany!
    With regret we left thy shore,
For like all the other countries
    We may never see thee more.

BELGIUM.

THIS was the last of all the eight
Of countries we had seen of late,
And as we entered Brussells town,
We looked around then up and down.

To see it was our intent,
On that our every mind was bent,
And much we saw upon that night
But more we saw by next day's light.

Our hotel, I forget its name,
But never mind, 'tis all the same,
It overlooked a busy street,
Where children, men, and women meet,

To talk and laugh in joyous glee,
As if they were from trouble free,
And yet 'tis work they have to do
Which lasts them 'til the day is through.

Brussells was pleasant in its way,
And yet we did not care to stay
For more than three days of the time,
Allotted us in foreign clime.

72

Next day we drove to public square,
There heard a story old and rare,
About the heroes of renown,
Who fought to settle that old town.

Heard much about the Belgian Lion,
And other things we could rely on,
Saw monuments and statues new,
And other things of beauty too.

"Palais of Justice" was gone through
Largest building the world can show,
Heard tale of this room and of that,
Then on the front steps down we sat.

And there a man our picture took,
A picture with a funny look,
For to laugh some felt inclined,
Others showed a serious mind.

Next drove to palace of the King,
There too was many a lovely thing,
As those which often we had seen,
Costly and rich with nothing mean.

Then to the hotel took our way,
To rest a little at mid-day,
In afternoon we shopped at ease,
If shopping did our fancy sieze,—

Or spent the time in resting some,
Or wrote to those we left at home,
Read over letters we'd received,
Found all were well and felt relieved.

That eve we went out with the guide,
Saw Brussells in its native pride,
And lovely gardens full of flowers,
Forming the most delightful bowers.

Brussells by night was very fine,
Where many, many lights did shine;
"Little Paris" so 'tis named,
And for its cleanliness is famed.

Next morn some went to Waterloo,
There the great Monument to view,
Of which in story all have read,
And know 'tis for the fallen dead.

Wirtz picture gallery was seen,
Unlike the others where we'd been,
The subjects were so very queer,
Some awful, others very drear.

That afternoon we spent at will,
Walking around or sitting still,
The evening passed in social way,
Or made ready for the coming day.

Next morn we bade our host adieu,
Shook hands with every one we knew,
Soon entered train, were on the way
To Antwerp, where our steamer lay.

HOMEWARD BOUND.

AT LAST we were assembled
On ship's deck once again;
This time it was the "Friesland"
That was to cross the main.

With fifteen hundred souls on board,
We started from the shore,
From Antwerp sailed at mid-day
With our party near three score.

The rain was falling fast that day
When we started from the land;
Our friends we left them cheering
For the little "Ackley Band."

As Belgium's shore receded,
Fair Holland came in view;
And in looking at its border,
We had all that we could do,

'Til the steward called to luncheon;
He knew just what to do,
For some of us felt hungry,
And some of us felt blue.

76

As night came on the clouds dispersed,
    And we could see the shore
Where many lights were flashing,
    Some thousands, less or more.

Our ship sped swiftly on her way,
    Soon entered the channel deep
Then the river Pilot left us,
    While we were fast asleep.

Next morn we arose refreshed,
    Those who felt quite well;
There were numbers not at breakfast,
    How many, I'll not tell.

Of the absent, Neptune had firm hold
    And held them in his grasp;
He's a hard old master, I am told,
    By those who sigh and gasp.

Most of the young folk ran around,
    Talked or laughed so gay;
Threw "bean-bags" at each other,
    Pronouncing it fine play;

Read stories climbed to bow-sprit,
    There seeking to explore
The mysteries of the "Friesland,"
    Seeking ever to know more.

Two days were used in voting
   For the coming President,
The first day Democratic,—
   Second, Republican went.

'Twas great fun to hear the speeches
   Made for the Democrat,
Hear the cheering oft repeated,
   See the waving of the hat.

And to see their grand procession,
   With their "rooster" held on high,
With America's flag a'floating,
   Singing, the "Sweet Bye and Bye."

The Republicans were not so loud
   In their demonstrations then ;
But when the votes were counted,
   They had beaten by a ten.

And so each day was full of fun,
   The weather being mild,
For all of us who felt quite well,
   The time was soon beguiled.

One day we called a meeting,
   And decided when on shore
We'd be known as the "Ackley Pilgrims,"
   From that time forever-more.

Each day did we consult the chart
　　To see how far away
Was our own dear and native land,
　　Our own America.

Sunday we all assembled
　　To hear the Gospel read;
In the dining-room we gathered,
　　And there our prayers we said.

Take the whole ten days together,
　　That we were out at sea,
I think it was as pleasant,
　　As an ocean trip could be.

But we had one little set-back,
　　As we neared our native land,
Which almost blanched the faces,
　　Of the little "Ackley Band."

The story spread that we must be
　　Held days in Quarantine;
As we had sailed from Antwerp
　　Where much cholera had been.

As we listened to the story,
　　Told with much interest,
We thought our luck had left us;
　　Or perhaps 'twas but a test—

Of our patience and endurance,
  Or at least we hoped 'twas so,
And that we should land in safety,
  With-out so much ado.

And no trouble did arise for us,
  Soon we were shaking hands
With friends who came to meet us
  From home, not foreign lands.

Thus closed our pleasant journey
  Across the ocean wide,
Thanks to Him who rules the universe
  And everything beside,

And thanks to our kind leader
  Who with never tiring zeal,
Smoothed over all rough places,
  If we did to him appeal.

Farewell to all who sailed with us
  Best wishes here I tender,
To every one I say farewell,
  And now my pen surrender.

ERRATUM.

Page 25; Third Stanza, last line, read (now) instead of "out."

Page 32; Last Stanza, insert word (long) in last line to read "Made many long years ago."

Page 40; Last Stanza, sixth line, word (clear) instead of "clean."

Page 46; First Stanza, seventh line, word (an) should be omited.

Page 72; Second Stanza, first line, insert the word (all) to read "To see all it was our intent."

Page 52; Fourth Stanza, last line, use word (seems) instead of "seemed."